Jem's Frog Fiasco

GOLDTOWN BEGINNINGS

★ ★ 2 ★ ★

Jem's Frog Fiasco

Susan K. Marlow
Illustrated by Okan Bülbül

Kregel
Publications

Jem's Frog Fiasco
© 2019 by Susan K. Marlow

Illustrations © 2019 by Okan Bülbül

Published by Kregel Publications, a division of Kregel Inc.,
2450 Oak Industrial Dr. NE, Grand Rapids, MI 49505.

ISBN 978-0-8254-4626-9, print
ISBN 978-0-8254-7626-6, epub

Printed in the United States of America
19 20 21 22 23 24 25 26 27 28 / 5 4 3 2 1

Contents

New Words

butcher—someone who cuts up and sells meat in a shop

cattails—tall plants with dark-brown velvety heads that grow in ponds

coop—a fenced area for chickens; a pen

coyote hole—a hole a miner digs in the ground or in a hillside to find gold

fiasco—something that turns out all wrong

froggin'—catching frogs

hoarse—when a person's voice sounds scratchy or croaky

lantern—a lamp with a handle for carrying

scraps—leftover food

stump—the bottom part of a tree left in the ground after the tree has been cut down

tuckered out—very tired

wilderness—a place where few people live; wild, rough country

CHAPTER 1

The Best Dog

A cold, wet nose jerked Jem Coulter awake.

Jem sat up and threw back his covers. "Nugget! How did you sneak in here?"

He looked around. Mama did not want their new dog inside the tent.

Not even if Nugget stayed clean. Not even if Jem's little sister, Ellie, asked a hundred times.

No sirree! Mama always shooed the dog outside.

Jem got dressed in a hurry. "Come on," he said. "Before Mama sees you."

Nugget's golden tail swished back and forth. He followed Jem through the tent flap and into the April sunshine.

Mama was sliding a pie into her big,

black cookstove. Smoke puffed out of the stovepipe. Bowls of dried blueberries sat on the work table.

Mama baked pies every Saturday. All the miners loved her pies.

So did the café owners, and everybody else in Goldtown.

Mama slipped two more pies in the oven. She shut the heavy iron door.

Then she turned around and put her hands on her hips. "How many times have I told you to keep that dog out of the tent?"

Jem's eyebrows went up. How did she know Nugget had sneaked inside?

"He woke me up," Jem explained. "He must have pushed open the tent flap."

"I think he had help." Mama smiled. "I saw your sister run off to the creek a minute ago."

Jem laughed. Leave it to Ellie to think of a way to wake him up.

He hugged Nugget. "You are the best dog. Even if Mama doesn't like to feed you."

Every day, Mama watched to make sure Jem didn't share his food with the fast-growing dog. She frowned when Nugget ate supper leftovers.

"The chickens should get those," she always said when Pa scraped the plates.

"They don't need Nugget's scraps," Pa told her. "They can eat grain and leftover mush."

Hurrah for Pa!

But even after three weeks of eating table scraps, Jem could still feel Nugget's sharp ribs.

After breakfast, Jem dumped a scoop of grain in the chicken coop. The rooster and five hens squawked and jumped out of the way.

Then they scratched the dirt to find every bit of food.

Jem grabbed his gold-mining pan and headed for his very own gold claim next to Cripple Creek.

He waved to Pa, who stood with their miner friend Strike-it-rich Sam.

Pa waved back. Then he grabbed the handle of a long wooden box and rocked it back and forth.

Strike dumped a bucket of dirt, water, and gravel into a big square hole on top.

The rocker box was supposed to make it easier to find gold.

So far, it hadn't worked very well.

Jem squatted next to the creek.

He scooped three handfuls of sand and
dirt into his pan. "I have to wash some gold
today. I just have to!"

He wanted to buy meat scraps for
Nugget. A young dog needed meat to grow.

Ellie sat down next to Jem. "Who are you
talking to?" She held a beat-up pie pan in
her lap—her gold pan.

"Just thinking out loud," Jem said.

"What about?"

Jem let out a big breath. A little sister could sure be a bother.

Especially when she asked questions all the time.

"Can't a miner pan for gold in peace?" he said.

Ellie didn't answer.

Instead, she watched Jem swirl his pan. She didn't pick up even one speck of dirt from her brother's gold claim.

Ellie knew the gold-camp rules.

Rule one and *rule two* went together. Stay on your own gold claim. Pan your own gold.

But there was no rule about keeping quiet.

"You didn't hit color last Saturday," Ellie said. "Or the Saturday before that."

"So what?"

"Maybe the gold's all gone."

"Roasted rattlesnakes, Ellie! Don't say that!"

Jem's heart thumped. No gold? Nugget would starve.

So would the Coulter family.

The miners would move away to look for

new diggings. Nobody would buy Mama's pies.

"You're good at panning gold," Ellie said. "Why else can't you find any?"

Good question.

"I don't know. Maybe I'm just unlucky, like No-luck Casey."

Casey couldn't find gold, no matter how hard he tried.

If he dug a coyote hole, he fell in and broke his leg. If the miner went prospecting, he got lost for days.

"That's me, No-luck Jem." He sighed.

"You can't use Casey's nickname," Ellie said. "He had it first."

Jem rolled his eyes. *Be quiet, Ellie*, he thought.

But he didn't say those words aloud. Mama would not like it if he snapped at his sister.

"If I can't find any gold," Jem said, "I'll think of a different way to buy meat scraps for Nugget."

Ellie wrinkled her eyebrows. "How?"

Jem shrugged. Then he got an idea.

An excellent idea.

"I'm going to find a job."

CHAPTER 2
A Job for Jem

All the way into Goldtown that afternoon, Jem thought about a job.

A job meant steady money. The gold he did find could stay in his pouch.

A job meant meat for Nugget. The butcher would save scraps and bones for Jem.

Tingles raced up and down his arms. *I'm big enough to find a job.*

Jem tugged on the wagon handle. "I know how to work," he said. "I have a job right now. I deliver pies for Mama."

"*We* deliver pies for Mama," Ellie said. "I keep the wagon from tipping over."

"I know." Jem pulled harder. "But you're slow as molasses."

Ellie hung on to the wagon's sides and walked faster.

Jem liked selling pies to the miners. He liked watching Mama's pouch grow lumpy with gold dust and gold nuggets.

Jem also liked seeing that mean rich boy, Will Sterling, run away from him.

Every Saturday, their new dog went to town with Jem and Ellie. Thanks to Nugget, mean Will stayed far away from their pie wagon.

Nugget didn't like Will. Not one bit. He growled at him every time.

Jem grinned. *Thank you, God, for Nugget.*

He was the best dog in all of California.

"What kind of job are you going to find?" Ellie asked.

Jem stopped thinking about Nugget. "I can do a lot of things."

"Like what?"

Jem had thought about jobs when he was panning for gold this morning. It was easy to wash gold and think at the same time.

Especially if no gold washed into his pan.

"I can run errands for the miners," he said. "I can fetch their coffee."

Ellie laughed. "Casey and Pearly Teeth and Strike fetch their own coffee."

Jem made a face. Ellie was right about that.

"Sweeping's a good job for a boy," he went on. "It's easy."

"What would you sweep?"

Jem huffed and didn't answer. Why did Ellie ask so many questions?

"I'm big enough to chop wood, too." He paused. "Maybe."

Pa let Jem split wood sometimes. But the ax was heavy.

Ellie shook her head. "You don't want to chop your fingers or toes off."

Jem wiggled his fingers. No, he might not be ready to chop wood, after all.

He pointed to the biggest canvas tent in Goldtown. "I might ask Mr. Tobias if I can run errands."

It was a noisy place. Men were always going in and out of that big tent.

Ellie gasped. "You can't run errands for a saloon."

"I can too."

"Pa and Mama would skin you alive."

Jem scowled at Ellie, but she was right. He did not want Pa or Mama to scold him.

A saloon was not a nice place.

Jem pulled the wagon to a stop in front of another large tent. Mama's last two pies were for Mr. Sims, the café owner.

"Mr. Sims!" Jem called.

There was no answer.

Jem picked up a blueberry pie. "Get the other one," he told Ellie.

If Mr. Sims was too busy to come outside, Jem and Ellie would go inside.

"Stay, Nugget," Jem said.

The golden dog flopped to the ground next to the wagon. His tail thumped the muddy ground.

"Good dog." Jem ducked through the doorway.

It was dark and smoky inside the café. Two oil lamps hung from the tent's canvas ceiling.

The smell of beef stew, biscuits, and beans made Jem's belly rumble. *Mmm!*

A lot of miners sat around the wooden tables. They laughed and talked and ate.

That part didn't smell as nice. Miners did not take baths very often.

When the men saw Jem and Ellie, they clapped and whooped.

"Fresh pies from the Coulter kids," No-luck Casey yelled. "I call the first slice."

How would Casey pay for a piece of pie? He never found any gold.

"Second piece!" another man shouted.

A young miner with curly hair helped himself to Ellie's pie. "I'll buy the whole pie."

"No!" Ellie shouted.

Mr. Sims came to the rescue. "Don't tease the kids, Jesse. Wait your turn."

The café owner took Ellie's pie. Then he took Jem's pie. He set them both down on the countertop.

He poured gold dust into Mama's pouch. "Your ma's pies are always a hit with my customers."

"Mr. Sims?" Jem's heart pounded.

It was now or never. "Do you need a boy to sweep up?"

Mr. Sims chuckled. "Look at the floor, Jem."

Jem glanced down. His face grew hot.

The café floor was dirt.

"I guess not." Jem sighed.

"You lookin' for a job?" Mr. Sims asked.

Jem's head popped up. "Yes, sir."

Mr. Sims crossed his arms over his chest. "You any good at catchin' those big bullfrogs?"

"I think so." Jem played at Bullfrog Pond when he didn't feel like panning for gold.

"Good." The café owner smiled. "I want to add frog legs to my menu."

He smacked his lips. "There's nothin' like fresh-caught, pan-fried frog legs. I'll pay you five cents a frog."

Jem's eyes opened wide. *Five cents a frog?* "Yes, sir!"

Jem made a promise to himself right then. He would become the best frog catcher in Goldtown.

Maybe in all the other California gold camps, too.

CHAPTER 3
Froggin'

Jem yanked on the wagon handle and ran.

The wagon bounced over ruts. The wheels bumped over big rocks in the road.

Empty pie pans rattled and banged inside the wagon.

Nugget ran back and forth, barking.

"Hurry up!" Jem yelled over his shoulder.

Ellie's short legs could not keep up. She ran a few more steps, then stopped.

Jem slowed down and turned around. "Ellie! What are you waiting for?" His breath came in short gasps. "Come on!"

"I can't run that fast."

Jem let out a big breath and waited.

He didn't want to wait. He wanted to run ahead and start catching frogs.

But he couldn't leave Ellie behind. Not even if she knew the way home.

Not even if Nugget stayed with her.

"What's the big hurry?" Ellie asked when she caught up.

"I want to go froggin'," Jem said. "Get in. I'll pull you home."

Ellie's sweaty face turned smiley. "Oh, boy!"

She climbed into the wagon.

"Hang on tight," Jem warned. "You don't want to bounce around like a pie pan."

Ellie giggled and grabbed the wagon's sides. "I'm ready."

Jem pulled on the handle. He went fast, but not as fast as he wanted to go.

The wagon might tip over. Ellie might fall out and get hurt. She'd cry, and Mama would scold.

Jem didn't have time to be scolded today. He wanted to catch frogs.

He slowed down even more when he got closer to home. The gold claims by Cripple Creek were full of dirt piles and big holes.

"Watch out for that coyote hole!" Ellie squealed and pointed.

"I see it."

Jem didn't know why the miners called their diggings *coyote holes*. No coyotes lived in them.

There was no gold in those holes either.

Panting, Jem pulled the wagon to a stop next to the work table. Mama was rolling out pie crusts.

"Mr. Sims gave me a job!" Jem shouted.

Ellie jumped out of the wagon. "Can we go to Bullfrog—"

"I'm telling this." Jem scowled at Ellie.

Ellie crossed her arms and scowled back. But she kept quiet.

Mama wiped her hands on her apron. "What kind of job?"

"He's going to pay me to catch frogs. Five cents each."

"My goodness," Mama said. "What will you do with so much money?"

Jem grinned. "I'll buy Nugget meat scraps. That way he won't be so hungry."

"That's a fine plan, Son," Mama said. "What would Nugget do without you?"

"I'm going to help," Ellie said. "I want to feed Nugget too."

Jem opened his mouth to say no, but Mama shook her head.

"Sure," he said with a big sigh.

Ellie clapped her hands. "Can we go right now?"

Mama looked at the pie crusts on the table. She glanced up at the sun.

Then she nodded. "You may go, but don't stay long. You have more pies to deliver this afternoon."

Jem whooped and went looking for a pail. He also found a flat piece of wood.

"What's the wood for?" Ellie asked.

"It's the lid to cover the pail," Jem said. "What good is catching frogs if they hop right out?"

Ellie looked at the pail. Then she looked at the lid. "I guess you know everything about catching frogs."

Jem laughed. "I guess I do."

Mama had something to say before Jem and Ellie ran off to Bullfrog Pond. "Look after your sister, Jeremiah. That pond can get deep."

"Yes, ma'am." Jem picked up the bucket and took Ellie's hand. "I won't let her drown."

Mama waved good-bye and turned back to her pies.

Hand in hand, Jem and Ellie took off for the pond.

Woof! Nugget leaped after them.

Bullfrog Pond was a long way upstream.

First, they crossed Cripple Creek. The water came up past Jem's knees.

Next, they pushed through scratchy bushes and tall grass.

Then they walked around oak trees and past tall pines.

Finally, Jem spied a clump of cattails. They grew along the edge of the pond.

He stopped. "Listen."

Ribbit, ribbit. Ribbit, ribbit.

The bullfrogs were croaking.

"They're loud," Ellie said. "And it sounds like there's a bunch of them."

Jem's heart gave a happy thump. So many frogs meant even more money!

He never thought a frog could be worth five cents. He added up the money in his head.

Twenty frogs would earn Jem a whole dollar.

He whistled. "We're going to be rich."

"Nugget will grow big and strong from all the meat scraps," Ellie said.

"He sure will." Jem stroked Nugget's head. "Won't you, fella?"

Woof! Nugget licked Jem's hand.

But would the miners really want to eat bullfrog legs at Mr. Sims's café?

Jem made a face. *Not me.*

A frog could be a pet, but it would never be his supper.

"Let's get closer," he told Ellie. "Frogs are slippery. They hop fast. You have to sneak up on them."

"I know." Ellie huffed. "I've caught frogs before."

"You've never caught a bullfrog before," Jem said. "They're big. Bigger than both your hands put together. Bigger even than—"

"Look!" Ellie pointed.

Jem stared. It was a bullfrog.

A big one.

CHAPTER 4

Cold and Wet

Jem's stomach flip-flopped. His first frog for money!

For a whole minute he stood still and watched the bullfrog. It sat right next to the water.

It didn't hop away. It didn't croak. It didn't even blink.

The frog looked sound asleep in the warm afternoon sunshine.

"It's taking a nap," Ellie said.

"Shh!" Jem put down the pail and crept closer. One step. Two steps.

Jem's heart pounded inside his chest. It beat so loud he was sure the frog could hear it.

Another step. Almost there.

31

Jem smiled. Catching this sleepy frog would be easy as pie.

The frog blinked.

Jem stopped short. He took a deep breath and held it.

"What are you waiting for?" Ellie tiptoed up beside him. She tugged on his sleeve. "Catch it."

Jem spun around. "Roasted rattlesnakes, Ellie! Bullfrogs have good ears." His voice came out in an angry whisper. "You'll scare it."

"Then hurry up and catch it before it hops away."

"Shh!" Jem turned back to the frog.

It was gone.

"That frog was perfect, and now it's gone." Jem kicked the mud. "You talk too much."

"I do not!"

Jem let out a big breath. "Where did it go?"

"I don't know."

Jem looked to the right. He looked to the left. He shaded his eyes and looked out across the pond.

A dragonfly swooped over his head. A mosquito buzzed.

But he couldn't see the frog.

"Ooh!" Ellie pointed. "I see it." She ran three steps and pounced on the frog.

Jem made his hands into tight fists. "No, Ellie. That's *my* frog!"

Too late.

Ellie curled her hands around the frog's belly. "I saw it first."

She lifted it out of the mud.

The frog was big. Maybe eight inches from head to toe. Its long legs hung down.

It looked slippery, too.

Ellie could not hold on. The frog began to slip through her fingers.

She squeezed tighter.

The frog opened its mouth and shrieked.

Jem nearly jumped a foot in surprise. He had never heard a bullfrog squeal.

The frog kept shrieking. It went on and on.

Ellie yelped and threw the frog at her brother.

Jem ducked. He didn't want to play catch with a screaming frog.

No sirree!

The frog flew over his head. *Plunk!* It landed on the ground in front of Nugget.

Nugget yipped and sprang into the air. All four paws left the ground.

When the golden dog landed, he circled the frog. He sniffed it and barked.

The frog sucked in air. It looked bigger than ever.

Worse, it blew out more squealing noises.

Ellie gasped.

Jem ran for his pail. Catching bullfrogs wasn't easy as pie, after all. It was almost time to go home, and he didn't even have one frog.

He had to catch this slippery hopper.

"I wish Mama would let me catch frogs by myself," he muttered.

Nugget was still circling the frog. He put his nose down and sniffed again.

Just then, the bullfrog took a big leap. It hopped past Jem, past Ellie, and past Nugget.

Plop! It landed in the water and started swimming.

That frog could swim fast! It swam away before Jem could catch it.

"Aren't you going after it?" Ellie asked.

Jem slumped. "I can't. The water's too deep."

The water was not too deep for Nugget. With one big jump, he leaped into the pond.

Splash! Water sprayed everywhere.

Drops splashed Jem's eyes and nose.

The water hit Ellie and soaked her hair. It dripped down her face.

"Nugget!" Jem wiped the water out of his eyes. "Come back here!"

Nugget did not obey. He was swimming fast.

But the bullfrog swam faster. Then it disappeared underwater.

Nugget stopped swimming. He looked surprised.

Where did that frog go?

Jem whistled and called Nugget.

Ellie called him too.

Finally, Nugget swam back to shore. He pulled himself out of the water and shook himself.

Water flew from his floppy ears and long tail. It flew from every hair on his body.

Jem and Ellie got wet all over again.

Ellie shivered. "I want to go home."

Jem wanted to go home too, but he didn't say so. "Oh, hush," he said in a grumpy voice. "Listen."

Ellie listened.

Jem listened too. He heard no croaking or splashing. No whirling dragonflies.

Not even a mosquito buzzed.

The water was full of puddle rings, where dozens of frogs had jumped in. Every bullfrog in Bullfrog Pond had vanished.

Just like that.

CHAPTER 5

Try, Try Again

Jem dragged his empty pail home.

It was a long walk. Long and cold. The sun had gone behind a cloud.

"All that work for nothing," Jem said when he and Ellie got home.

"Not even one frog?" Mama looked like she was trying hard not to smile.

"Nope." Jem dropped the pail on the ground. "Nugget scared them all away."

"Cheer up, Son," Pa said. "Froggin' is best done at night, during a full moon." He ruffled Jem's hair. "You'll catch a bucketful of hoppers if you use a lantern."

Jem cheered right up. "When is the next full moon?"

Pa thought hard. "In two weeks."

Two weeks? Jem needed to sell frogs sooner than that.

"Jem is not going to that pond in the middle of the night," Mama told Pa. "Unless you go with him."

Jem slumped. Daytime froggin' would have to do for now.

Mama kept Jem and Ellie busy the rest of the afternoon.

They pulled the pie wagon to town. They sold more pies.

Jem stayed busy all week, too.

Mama and Ellie washed the miners' clothes every morning. Jem delivered the clean laundry after school.

Jem also did other chores. He filled the wood box clear to the top. He brushed Nugget. He cleaned out the chicken coop.

Jem could hardly wait until Saturday, when he could go froggin' again.

· ★ ★ ★ ·

On Saturday, Jem gobbled his morning mush. He wanted to get an early start to the pond.

For sure he would catch frogs today. A *lot* of frogs.

"Come here, Nugget." He whistled for his dog.

Nugget came running.

Jem found a rope and tied Nugget to a bush. "You're not coming. You'll scare away every frog in the pond."

Nugget whined, but Jem shook his head. "You'll chase them all underwater again."

"I'm coming." Ellie held up a rusty bucket. "Strike gave me a frog pail."

Jem groaned. "All right. But you better keep quiet and do what I say."

Ellie nodded happily.

"Look after your sister," Mama called as Jem and Ellie set out.

"I will," Jem promised.

The creek was freezing cold this morning. Jem held Ellie's hand and waded across as fast as he could.

"Brrr!" Ellie shivered.

Jem and Ellie warmed up when they ran through the tall grass and around the oak trees.

By the time Jem reached the pond, he was

hot and sweaty. The sun shone down on the
still, blue water.

The bullfrogs were croaking as loud as
ever.

Jem put a finger to his lips and tiptoed
through the squishy mud. He pushed apart
the cattails and looked down.

His mouth fell open.

A whopper of a hopper sat right at his feet. Nine inches long, at least.

"Mr. Sims will sure be happy," he whispered to Ellie.

Quick as a wink, Jem pounced. He grabbed the frog just above its back legs and held on tight. "Got it!"

The bullfrog didn't have time to wiggle. It didn't have time to shriek.

Jem plopped the frog in his pail and dropped the lid on top. "Now he can't jump out."

He looked at Ellie. "That was easy."

Ellie's eyes were big and full of surprise. "It sure was."

She squatted next to Jem's pail and lifted the board.

"Don't you dare let that frog go," Jem said.

"I won't. I just want to see it."

Jem squatted next to Ellie and peeked inside the pail. Two huge, dark eyes stared up at him.

He whistled. "It's a beauty, isn't it?"

Ellie nodded. Then her mouth opened wide. "Oh, look!"

She pointed at another—even bigger—bullfrog. It sat halfway in the water.

Cattails hid most of it. Only its huge head and neck showed.

And its eyes. Big bullfrog eyes.

"I'll get it," Ellie whispered.

Jem grabbed her arm. "No, let me. I'm bigger. You don't know how."

"I do too!" Ellie stood up.

"What if it screams? You dropped the last one, remember?"

Ellie pulled her arm away. "I found it. I'm going to catch it."

Before Jem could stop her, Ellie waded into the shallow water. She reached for the frog.

Jem gasped. Ellie was quick. Nearly as quick as he was.

She pulled the frog out of the water and held it up. "See?"

Jem felt his eyes bug out. It was a monster bullfrog. Even bigger than the frog in his pail.

"Hurry!" he shouted. "Drop it in the pail."

Too late.

The frog squirmed. It wiggled. It kicked both back legs. But it did not shriek.

Instead, it bit Ellie.

Ellie's scream echoed across the pond. She threw her hands up in the air.

The frog flew higher.

Then *plop!* It dropped into the pond and swam away.

Ellie splashed out of the water. "It bit me!"

"Roasted rattlesnakes!" Jem yelled. "Stop crying. You're scaring away the frogs."

Ellie cried louder and held up her finger. "Look. Bite marks. It hurts."

Jem did not want to look at his sister's finger. He didn't want to listen to her sobs. He didn't want her to help catch frogs.

"You're making too much noise!" he yelled.

"So are you!"

Ellie was right about that, but Jem was too mad to care. "You're too little to catch frogs."

"I'm *not* too little!" Ellie howled.

"You're not catching any more frogs with me." Jem pointed to the pail. "You sit right there until I'm done."

"No."

"Do what I tell you," Jem said. "Or you can go home."

"You're mean and bossy." Ellie's shrieks grew louder. "As mean as that rich boy, Will Sterling."

Sobbing, she turned and stomped away.

CHAPTER 6

Frogs and More Frogs

Jem's hands curled into tight fists. "Come back here!"

"No!" Ellie did not turn around. She didn't come back. She just kept walking.

At least she was headed home.

Good. Jem let out an angry breath. Sometimes it was hard being the big brother.

"Good-bye!" he yelled after her.

Ellie didn't answer.

Jem watched Ellie push through the tall grass. He listened until he couldn't hear her cries anymore.

Then everything grew quiet.

The frogs didn't croak. No birds sang. The cattails didn't even rustle.

Jem tried to feel cheerful. He was getting his wish. He could catch frogs all by himself now.

Then some not-so-cheerful thoughts sneaked into his head. *You should not have yelled at Ellie. It was unkind.*

Jem's belly flip-flopped. *Mama won't like it.*

No, Mama wouldn't like it at all.

Her words whispered in his head. *"Look after your sister."*

Jem had promised he would. His belly did another flip.

When Ellie got home, she would tell Mama what happened.

Then Mama would send Ellie back to the pond with a message: Come home *right now.*

Trouble with a capital T.

Jem shaded his eyes and looked for Ellie. "I better go after her," he mumbled.

But the thick bushes and tall grass blocked his view. He couldn't see her anymore. He couldn't hear her.

Ellie was gone. She was probably halfway home by now.

Jem sat down next to his pail. "Never mind," he told the frog. "I'll find out soon enough if Ellie tattles on me."

Until then? Jem might as well catch some more frogs.

He found a shady place to wait. If he waited long enough, the frogs would come back.

A few minutes went by. Then more minutes went by.

Jem peeked inside the pail. The bullfrog looked up at him with unblinking eyes.

It looked unhappy.

Jem carried the pail to the edge of the pond. He splashed water on the frog.

Then he sat down and waited some more.

The pond sparkled in the sun. Water bugs raced across the surface. A fish jumped.

A long time later, Jem heard croaking.

He smiled. The bullfrogs had settled down after their terrible fright.

His own thoughts had settled down too. Ellie was probably home. If she had told Mama, Jem would know it by now.

Ellie would have come back. She would have scared the frogs all over again.

Jem let out a happy sigh. Ellie was not a tattletale.

He was *very* sorry he'd yelled at her. He would tell her so when he went home.

But first he would fill his bucket with hoppers.

Another thought cheered him up even more. "I'll give Ellie one of the frogs for a pet. She loves pets."

Happy with his idea to make up with Ellie, Jem put his mind on catching frogs.

The croaking grew louder. The bullfrogs were calling to each other. More and more began to answer back.

Jem sat still as a stone and waited.

He was used to waiting. He got a lot of practice. Panning for gold took a long time.

Nearly as long as catching frogs.

Jem looked up. The sun was climbing higher in the sky. It was time to go after those frogs.

Jem didn't make a sound when he stood up. Tiptoeing, he crept to the cattails and peeked in the water.

There! He caught his breath. And over there! Another one.

The frogs looked like they were napping.

They must be croaking in their sleep, Jem thought.

He sneaked up on the first bullfrog. He grabbed it before it could hop or swim away.

Plop! He dropped it into his bucket—right on top of the first frog.

It took no time to catch three more frogs.

Plop! Plop! Plop! Into the pail they went.

The frogs kept trying to escape. They could push hard. The lid popped off.

"No!" Jem put a big rock on the board to hold it down.

Then he went back to froggin'.

Soon, Jem's pail was filled to the top. Eight bullfrogs for Mr. Sims!

Jem tried to lift the pail, but it was too heavy. He tried again. No good.

One or two frogs would have to be left behind.

He tossed the two smallest hoppers back in the pond. They swam away fast.

Jem sighed. "I sure wish Ellie was here." She could help him carry the pail.

He worked hard to lug the pail of frogs home.

Carrying that pail was harder than carrying firewood. It was harder than hauling water for Mama.

The frogs were jumpy, too. They wanted to hop out of the pail.

Every few minutes, Jem had to stop. He had to grab a frog and put it back in the pail.

"For sure I'll use the wagon to take them

to Mr. Sims," Jem said. "I can't carry this bucket all the way to Goldtown."

The sun was high in the sky by the time Jem got home.

He dropped the bucket on the ground next to the family tent. Then he found a big rock to hold the lid down.

He sniffed. Cornbread and beans for lunch. *Mmm!*

"Look at all my frogs," he told Mama. "That's thirty whole cents."

Mama turned around from the cook-stove. She didn't look at the frogs.

She looked at Jem and wrinkled her eyebrows. "Where is your sister?"

CHAPTER 7
Missing

Jem's happy smile faded. Ellie?

"She's here." He swallowed. "Isn't she?"

"No, she's not," Mama said. "I haven't seen either of you since you took off for the frog pond."

Jem looked around the claim. Nugget was still tied up.

When Nugget saw Jem, he whined and wagged his tail.

Let me loose, he seemed to be saying.

Six pies sat on the work table. A pot of beans simmered on the stovetop. Next to the beans, a pan of cornbread cooled.

Suddenly, Jem wasn't hungry.

He shaded his eyes. Down at the creek, Pa

was working on the rocker box with Strike. Rocks and gravel clattered down the inside of the box and fell into the water.

But Ellie was nowhere in sight.

Thump, thump, thump. Jem's heart beat harder than a hammer inside his chest.

His throat felt tight, like a lump was stuck there. He couldn't get one word past that lump.

"Well?" Mama put her hands on her hips. "Where is she?"

Mama sounded worried. And angry.

"Look after your sister." Her words spun around in Jem's mind.

He ducked his head. *I didn't keep my promise*, he thought.

Jem swallowed the lump in his throat.

"Me and Ellie got in a big fight," he said in a small voice. "She was scaring away all the frogs. I told her to go home."

Jem did not tell Mama that he'd yelled at Ellie. He didn't tell her that he'd been bossy and unkind.

He didn't have to. Mama was a good guesser.

"You promised to look after her," she said sadly.

A sob caught in Jem's throat. Mama sounded so disappointed.

Then a new thought made Jem's belly burn. "I bet she's hiding, just to get me in trouble."

"You had better hope she is, Jeremiah."

Jem squirmed. Mama called him Jeremiah when she was upset. Or when he was in trouble.

"Go ask Pa to come here," Mama said.

"Pa?" Jem's heart beat even faster.

Mama nodded. "Hurry."

Now he was really in trouble. "Yes, ma'am."

Jem turned and ran as fast as he could. Tears stung his eyes. Where could Ellie be?

By the time Jem reached the creek, he had sniffed back his tears. Not one drop leaked out.

But his belly would not settle down. His hands shook. "Pa!"

Pa and Strike turned around.

"We found a mighty fine nugget, Son." Pa grinned. "What do you think about that?"

"Mama wants you," Jem said, panting. "Ellie's missing."

Crash! Pa dropped his bucket. Rocks and gravel plunked into the creek. *"What?"*

"Go on, Matt," Strike said. "Find out what happened. The young'un can't be far."

Pa grabbed Jem's hand. They rushed back to the tent.

Mama told Pa the whole story. It didn't take long.

When she finished, she wiped her eyes with a corner of her apron.

Pa hugged her. "Don't worry, Ellen. We'll find her."

"I still think she's hiding," Jem whispered. "She'll come home when she gets hungry."

But Jem did not believe his own words.

The gold fields were big. The forests around the gold fields were even bigger.

Strike was always telling stories about the wilderness.

It was easy to get lost. A miner could walk around in circles for days and never find his way back to camp.

At least, that's what Strike said.

Jem's heart was really pounding now. A little girl could easily lose her way.

And then there were the bobcats and mountain lions and bears and—

Jem's hands shook. "She's hiding."

Ellie *must* be hiding. She had to be!

Pa sat down on a stump and pulled Jem onto his lap. "Were you not told to look after your sister?"

Jem nodded.

"If she was being too noisy, why didn't you bring her back home to Mama?"

Jem squirmed. He knew why, but he didn't want to tell Pa.

Jem had not wanted to take the time to bring Ellie home. He wanted to catch frogs.

The lump in his throat came back. His eyes stung. "I told her to do what I said, or she could go home."

Pa frowned at Jem. Then he looked at Mama.

Mama's face was white. "She's so little, Matt. Where can she be?"

Pa lifted Jem's chin and looked in his eyes. "How long ago, Jeremiah?"

Jem scrunched up his forehead, thinking hard. "The sun was about halfway to noon," he said.

Mama gasped. "That was over two hours ago." She started crying.

That scared Jem even more. He wished Mama would scold him. He wished Pa would paddle him.

They did neither.

Pa lifted Jem off his lap and stood up. "I'll round up some men. We'll find her."

Mama wiped her eyes and nodded.

Jem stood still. His thoughts spun. *No. I'll find her.*

Ellie was hiding. He was sure of it.

But where?

CHAPTER 8

Hide-and-Seek

"I want to look for Ellie too," Jem said. "I know all her favorite hiding places."

Pa smiled. "That's a good idea, Son."

The scolding was over—for now. It looked like Pa didn't have time to really get after Jem.

That would come later. Right now, it was more important to find Ellie.

Jem did not smile back. *This is my fault*, he thought.

He was the big brother. A big brother watched out for his little sister.

Even when he didn't want to.

A new idea found its way into Jem's head. Ellie was hiding, but maybe she'd fallen asleep in her hiding place.

No wonder she hadn't come home! Jem would find her and bring her back.

"But where should I look first?" he asked himself.

A cheerful thought made his feet fly. That old fallen log! It was so big that—

Ribbit, ribbit.

Jem stopped short. *Uh-oh.*

The bullfrogs were calling. They wanted out of their pail.

"I need to take my frogs to Mr. Sims," Jem said. "Then I'll look for Ellie."

Pa shook his head. "It will take too long."

Pa was right about that.

"I can't keep them in the bucket," Jem said. "They'll die."

"That's true," Pa said. He pointed to Cripple Creek. "Dump the frogs in the creek."

Jem bit his lip. "All of them?"

"Every last one."

"Yes, sir."

Jem lifted the heavy pail with both hands. He walked to the creek and tipped the bucket onto its side.

"Good-bye, hoppers," he said with a sigh. "Good-bye, thirty cents."

Splash! Six bullfrogs leaped into the water.

Jem watched the frogs swim away. Tears stung his eyes, but he didn't cry.

He knew a punishment when he saw one.

When every last frog had disappeared under the water, Jem stood up. He glanced back at his family's camp.

Pa was gone. Mama was gone.

They were looking for Ellie.

"I better look too," Jem said.

He left his frog bucket on the rocks. Then he found his boots and laced them up.

Soon, he was running through the oak and pine woods. "Ellie!"

There was no answer.

Jem ran faster. He dashed all the way to a huge log that lay in the woods.

Years ago, a giant pine tree had fallen to the ground. It happened long before Jem was born. Or even Pa.

The inside of the tree had rotted. Now, the log was hollow.

Jem and Ellie liked to play hide-and-seek in there.

Ellie sometimes liked to play tea party in the log.

One time, she found a baby bunny. She gave the bunny its own cracked teacup.

Jem wrinkled his nose. *Girls!*

Maybe Ellie was not asleep. Maybe she was playing tea party today.

Jem crawled inside the hollow log. There was plenty of room. "Ellie?"

Ellie wasn't inside the log. But a bunch of black ants were.

Jem left in a hurry. He didn't like ants. Their bites felt like little pinches.

"Maybe she went back to the pond." He frowned. "She might be hiding in the cattails. Or in the bushes on the other side."

It didn't take Jem long to get to the pond. He ran most of the way.

"Ellie!" he shouted. "Come out. I'm sorry I yelled at you."

The bullfrogs stopped croaking. Jem's loud voice had scared them underwater.

Jem didn't care. He pushed the cattails apart. "Ellie, where are you?"

She didn't answer.

Jem walked all the way around the pond. He looked behind every bush, but he didn't find Ellie.

High in the sky, a hawk glided on the breeze.

"I wish I was you," Jem called. "Then I could fly over the wilderness and see where Ellie went."

He sat down on a log and thought.

But not for long. It was getting late. The sun was sinking lower in the sky.

Jem ran as fast as he could to check two other hiding places in the woods.

Ellie was not in either place.

There was only one other spot where Ellie might be hiding. She liked to play in Strike's tent. It was small and cozy.

Maybe Ellie had sneaked in there to hide when nobody was looking.

Another thought sent Jem racing back to

Strike's camp. "Maybe she fell asleep inside the tent."

His thoughts buzzed like a swarm of bees. Of course! Ellie was asleep in Strike's tent!

His boots pounded the ground. *Hurry, hurry!*

Jem ran out of the woods. Then he stopped and shaded his eyes.

Strike's tent stood on the other side of Cripple Creek. A fire burnt inside a circle of rocks in front of the tent.

Strike sat next to the fire drinking a cup of coffee.

"Yoo-hoo!" Jem called. "Strike!" He waved his arms.

His miner friend waved back at him. "Any luck, young'un?"

Jem splashed through the water and joined Strike. His breath came in little gasps. He was so tired, he could hardly talk.

He pointed to the tent. "Is Ellie inside?"

"Nope." Strike put down his cup. "I poked my head inside a minute or two ago. Didn't see her."

Tears pooled in Jem's eyes. Ellie wasn't hiding. She was really and truly lost.

CHAPTER 9

Coyote Holes

"I can't find Ellie anywhere," Jem told Strike.

His voice came out shaky.

"Sit down, young'un." Strike patted a big rock. "Rest a spell. You're all tuckered out."

Strike sounded calm. Like always. Nothing ever seemed to bother the old miner.

Not even a missing little girl.

Jem plopped down on the rock and rubbed his eyes. He sniffed and tried to make the tears stop.

But he couldn't stop them. They dripped down his cheeks.

I'm sorry, God, he prayed. *I didn't look after Ellie. Please help me find her.*

"Don't worry." Strike's rough hand squeezed Jem's shoulder. "Everybody's out searching."

Jem looked around.

The miners usually panned gold on both sides of Cripple Creek. Now, the creek banks were empty. Gold pans, picks, and shovels lay scattered on the rocks.

Jem looked up. The sun was going down fast.

His belly felt like a tight knot. "It's getting late. What can I do?"

"Well . . ." Strike scratched his whiskers. "Looks to me like you've done everything you could."

He nodded at Nugget. "Why don't you let Nugget try?"

At the sound of his name, the golden dog rose. *Woof!*

"Let him sniff a doll," Strike said. "Or Ellie's clothes."

Jem wrinkled his forehead. "Nugget doesn't know where she is."

"Doesn't matter," Strike said. "That dog's got a good nose. And he's smart. He might sniff her out."

Strike shrugged. "It sure can't hurt to try."

He was right about that.

The tight knot in Jem's stomach melted. "Why didn't somebody think of Nugget sooner?"

"I did, but nobody was around to tell," Strike said. "Your pa asked me to stay here in case Ellie came back on her own."

He paused. "Now, get going."

Jem leaped to his feet. He no longer felt tired. He felt full of energy. This was something he could do!

He untied Nugget. "Come on, boy."

Jem raced inside the Coulter family's large canvas tent. Nugget followed.

It didn't take long to find Ellie's beat-up rag doll. The doll was missing a button eye and some of her yarn hair.

But Molly was Ellie's favorite—and only—doll.

Jem held Molly under Nugget's nose.

Nugget sniffed the doll and gave a happy bark. He liked Ellie.

"Find Ellie," Jem said.

Nugget cocked his head and looked at him.

Jem pushed the doll closer to Nugget's nose. "Find Ellie." He pointed outside. "Go!"

Nugget ran through the tent flap. Once outside, he put his nose to the ground.

The dog circled the tent two times. Then he ran to Strike's tent. He went inside and came out.

Jem hurried to catch up.

When Nugget stopped, Jem put Molly to the dog's nose. "Find Ellie."

Nugget sniffed the ground and took off toward the creek.

"Wait for me!" Jem hurried after his dog.

"That's one smart pup!" Strike hollered. "Be careful, young'un."

Jem barely heard his miner friend. He was too busy splashing across Cripple Creek.

Nugget waited on the other side. He put his nose to the ground and ran along the creek bank.

Up and down the creek he went. He stopped, but not for long. He bounded away, toward the pond.

Jem was panting by the time he reached Bullfrog Pond. "Nugget! Where are you?"

Woof! Nugget burst out from the bushes. When he saw Jem, he ran past the pond and toward the woods.

"Wait!" Jem's foot caught on a big root. Down he went. *Ouch!*

Nugget came back. His cold, wet nose pushed against Jem's face. He sniffed the rag doll and barked.

Come on, he seemed to be saying. *Hurry!*

Nugget waited for Jem to get up. Then he leaped away.

A long time later, Nugget led the way into a big clearing.

Jem stopped. His mouth fell open.

He had never seen this place before. It looked like a bunch of old gold claims.

Dirt and rocks lay heaped in piles. A steep hill rose on the other side of the clearing.

The miners had dug a lot of coyote holes in that hill.

The ground was full of coyote holes, too.

Jem peeked into the hole by his foot. It didn't look like anybody had found gold down there.

He looked around. It didn't look like anybody had found gold in any of these coyote holes.

If the miners had found gold, they would have stayed and dug a real gold mine. Like rich Will Sterling's father had.

Mr. Sterling owned a new mine up on Belle Hill. It even had a name—the Midas Mine.

Somebody's old coyote hole had sure hit color up on Belle Hill.

But not here. Jem had never seen so many coyote holes in one place.

No gold, though.

Nugget barked. Jem looked up.

The dog's nose was pressed to the ground. He ran this way and that.

Then he stopped beside a coyote hole and barked. His tail wagged.

Jem dashed around two coyote holes. He ran past three piles of dirt and rocks.

When he reached Nugget, Jem peeked over the edge of the hole.

"Ellie!"

CHAPTER 10

Lost and Found

Thank you, God! Jem prayed.

He stuffed Molly in his waistband. Then he squatted next to Nugget.

"Good dog. You found Ellie." He hugged him tight.

Nugget's tail thumped. He licked Jem's cheek.

"Ellie!" Jem shouted.

Ellie didn't answer. She didn't move. She lay at the bottom of the coyote hole.

Jem leaned over the edge for a closer look. Why didn't Ellie answer? Was she asleep? Or—

No! Jem squeezed his eyes shut. *Please, God, she can't be hurt bad.*

He opened his eyes and yelled as loud as he could. "Ellie! Wake up! Please wake up!"

Ellie woke with a sob. She looked up. "Jem?"

"I'm here, Ellie. Nugget found you." Jem grinned. "He's the best dog in the whole—"

"Get me out of here!" Ellie cried. "I want Mama."

Jem wrinkled his eyebrows in surprise.

Ellie's voice sounded funny. Like she had a sore throat. Or like she had yelled herself hoarse.

She probably yelled for hours and hours, Jem thought.

Ellie was sobbing now. It was a tired sob. Not at all like her usual loud cries.

She sounded all worn out.

Her face was dirty and streaked with tear stains.

Poor Ellie!

"I'm sorry you're in this fix," Jem said. "I'm sorry I yelled at you."

Ellie didn't say, *"I forgive you."* She didn't say, *"That's all right."*

She just kept crying. "Get me out of here!"

"I will," Jem promised.

The hole was not as deep as Jem first thought. But it was over Ellie's head. And the sides were steep and crumbly.

No wonder she couldn't climb out.

"Stop crying and stand up," Jem said. "Show me how high you can reach."

Ellie stood up and raised her arms. Her hands were black with dirt. So was her dress.

For sure she had tried to climb out of the hole.

"You're sure brave." Jem didn't know why he said those words, but Ellie stopped crying.

"Mostly I'm hungry," she said. "And scared. But not as scared as I was when I fell in."

Jem flopped onto his belly. He scooted over the edge until his hands hung down.

He reached into the coyote hole as far as he could. "Grab my hands."

"I can't."

Jem bit his lip. "Maybe I should run home and get Pa."

"Nooo!" Ellie shouted. "Get me out of here!"

Jem thought hard. "Stand on your tiptoes."

Ellie stood on her tiptoes and reached high.

Jem grabbed her hands. His hands were sweaty.

"Make me strong, God," he prayed. He took a deep breath and pulled.

Ellie was heavy, but Jem didn't let go. He slid up onto his knees and pulled harder.

Ellie's belly slid over the edge of the hole. "Ow!"

Jem stood up. He yanked Ellie farther

away from the hole. Then he helped her stand up.

"I'm sorry." He hugged her tight.

Ellie hugged him back. Then they both hugged Nugget.

"You're a real hero," Jem told the dog. "Wait till Pa and Mama hear about this."

He took Ellie's hand. "It's a long way home, and it's getting dark. We better go."

Jem didn't ask Ellie how she ended up in a coyote hole so far from the pond.

He didn't have to. Ellie did all the talking.

"I was so mad, I just ran and ran," she said. "Then I got lost. I heard a noise and got scared. I tripped and fell down that ol' coyote hole."

Ellie chattered faster than a chipmunk.

Jem rolled his eyes. *She sure likes to talk.* He held Ellie's hand and let her talk.

He held her hand all the way home.

A Peek into the Past: Coyote Holes

Miners called the holes they dug *coyote holes*. They named the holes after coyote dens. Maybe they thought the holes they dug looked like coyote dens.

Coyotes dig their dens in hillsides or steep banks. A prospector dug his hole in a hillside, a steep bank, or straight down in the ground.

Sometimes coyotes dig shallow dens, only three feet underground. At other times, they dig dens six feet underground.

Like a coyote den, a miner's hole could be

shallow or deep. Some miners' coyote holes were one hundred feet deep!

Prospectors dug coyote holes to find gold. A shallow hole meant the prospector had given up quickly when he didn't find any gold.

A deep coyote hole showed that a prospector had tried harder. Or maybe he had found just enough gold to keep him hopeful of hitting a big strike.

Deep coyote holes were very narrow. There was usually only enough room for one man and his pick. He broke off the hard-packed clay and dirt.

Then a bucket was lowered into the hole, and the miner filled it up. After that, he had to find water to wash the dirt away and pan the gold.

So much work for so little gold.

* ★ ★ ★ ·

Download free coloring pages and learning activities at GoldtownAdventures.com.